盜夢者

Dreamstealer

Written by Elaine Joseph

Illustrated by Maggie Raynor

Chinese translation by Sylvia Denham

Mantra

「坐穩些，艾利，讓我看看你斷了的腿。」美瑾對她心愛的玩具說道。

「來呀，女孩子，」媽媽説。「今天我肯定你會是一位獸醫，但現在是時間上床睡覺了。」

"Sit still Elly and let me look at your broken leg," Megan said to her favourite toy.
"Come girl," Mum said. "One day I am sure you will be a vet, but right now it's time for bed."

那天晚上美瑾造夢，見到自己正在照顧
很多生病的動物和令牠們好轉。

That night Megan dreamt she was taking
care of many sick animals and making
them better.

突然,一隻凶猛的動物走進她
的夢境裡。

Suddenly, into her dream came a
fierce creature.

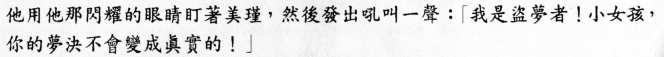

他用他那閃耀的眼睛盯著美瑾，然後發出吼叫一聲：「我是盜夢者！小女孩，你的夢決不會變成真實的！」

He fixed his glittering eyes on Megan, then let out a roar:
"I am the Dreamstealer! Your dream, little girl,
will never come true!"

他把美瑾的夢撈進網中，
並飛出窗外，而夢則努力
地掙扎，企圖擺脫。

He scooped up Megan's
dream into a net and flew out
of the window, with the
dream struggling to break free.

他把夢帶回他那位於月亮黑暗那一邊的堡壘，
並將它鎖進盜夢室。
「世界上所有的夢很快便會全屬於我的了！」
他一邊笑道，一邊搔抓著他的癢瘡。

He took it back to his castle on the
dark side of the moon and locked
it in the Room of Stolen Dreams.
"Soon all the dreams in the
world will be mine!"
he laughed, scratching
his boils.

第二天，美瑾整天感到不安和發牢騷地說她失去了一些東西。
「究竟甚麼事？」媽媽溫和地問。「你的樣子那麼悲哀，所有光彩
都離你而去了。」

The next day Megan felt miserable and
grumbled she had lost something.
"What's the matter?" Mum asked gently. "You
look so sad. All the sparkle has gone out of you."

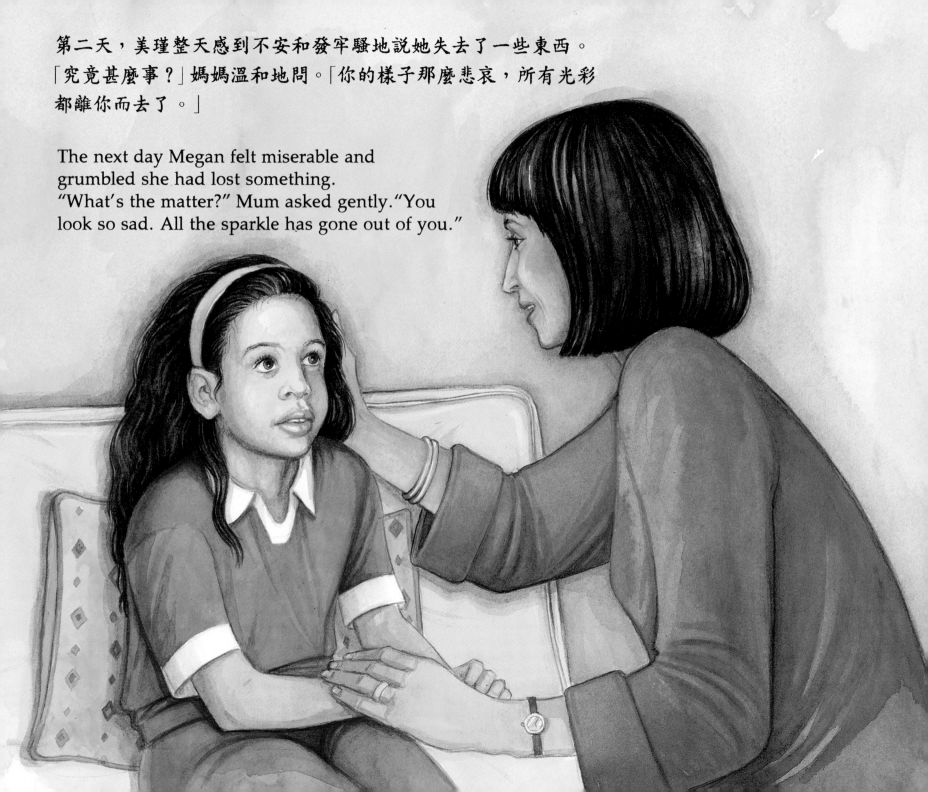

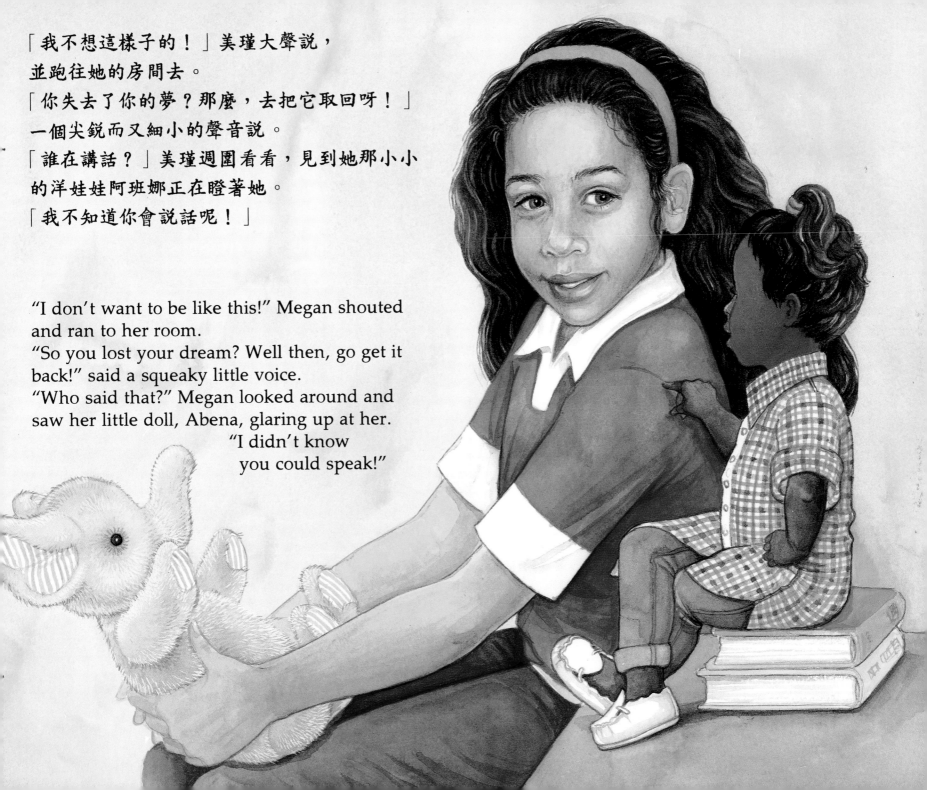

「我不想這樣子的！」美瑾大聲說，
並跑往她的房間去。
「你失去了你的夢？那麼，去把它取回呀！」
一個尖銳而又細小的聲音說。
「誰在講話？」美瑾週圍看看，見到她那小小
的洋娃娃阿班娜正在瞪著她。
「我不知道你會說話呢！」

"I don't want to be like this!" Megan shouted
and ran to her room.
"So you lost your dream? Well then, go get it
back!" said a squeaky little voice.
"Who said that?" Megan looked around and
saw her little doll, Abena, glaring up at her.
                    "I didn't know
                      you could speak!"

「我沒有時間去解釋，是盜夢者，是他偷走了你的夢。你要把它取回。」

「但是他很凶猛，我很害怕，」美瑾說。

「我有希望，你有希望，每個人都有少許的希望，就帶這些星塵和繩索去幫你，」阿班娜回答道。

"I don't have time to explain. The Dreamstealer is the one. He stole your dream. You have to get it back."

"But he's so fierce. I'm scared," said Megan.

"I got hope, you got hope, everybody got a little bit of hope. Here, take this stardust and rope to help you," answered Abena.

「現在撒一些星塵，許一個願，然後
跟著你的願望途徑走。」
美瑾撒出星塵，然後許願，再許願。
突然在她的眼前出現一條小徑。她小心踏上
小徑，帶著繩索，走向盜夢者的堡壘。

"Now throw some stardust and make a
wish, then follow the path of your wish."
Megan threw the stardust and wished and
wished. Suddenly there before her eyes
was a path. She stepped carefully onto it
and taking the rope, she ran towards the
Dreamstealer's castle.

穿過那些大閘，

Through the big gates,

橫過一個庭院，並……

across the courtyard...

走進大堂，盜夢者正坐在桌子上，沉沉睡著。

into the main hall, where at a table sat
the Dreamstealer, fast asleep.

美瑾看見一些鎖匙，於是指揮繩索將她舉到桌上去。

Megan saw some keys and commanded the rope to lift her onto the table.

她迅速地抓緊鎖匙，
由一個門口跑到另一個門口，
尋找盜夢室。

She quickly grabbed the keys and
ran from door to door looking for
the Dream Room.

她突然見到它！
於是把繩索變成梯級，然後
跑上去將鎖匙放到門上，
把門鎖開啓。

Suddenly she saw it!
Turning the rope into stairs, she
ran up them, put the key in the
door and unlocked it.

她推開盜夢室的門，然後……

She pushed open the door
of the Dream Room
and…

…停下來。整個房間放滿夢啊！
有些夢正在呻吟，有些則好像迷失方向失去了記憶的。當它們見到
美瑾時，夢境中的兒童叫道：「放我們出去呀！放我們出去呀！」

…stopped. The whole room was full of dreams!
Some dreams were moaning, others looked lost and forgotten. When they
saw Megan, the children in the dreams cried, "Let us out! Let us out!"

美瑾走進房間，推開窗門，
並把所有夢都放走了。
她那麼忙碌，連盜夢者正在醒過
來也聽不到。

Megan ran across the room, threw the windows open
and set the dreams free. She was so busy she didn't hear the
Dreamstealer waking up.

盜夢者打了個呵欠和伸一
下懶腰，他突然看到在黑
暗的房間中有一度閃耀著
的星塵。「誰人在我的堡
壘內？」他大聲吼叫。

The Dreamstealer yawned
and stretched and suddenly
in the dark room he saw the
trail of glittering stardust.
"WHO'S IN MY CASTLE?"
he roared.

當他由一個門口走到另一個門口時，
他那沉重的腳蹄轟隆地穿過大堂，
他用他那火辣的噴氣，把門都
燒掉了。

His heavy hooves boomed
through the great hall as he
went from door to door and
with his fiery breath he
burned them all down.

美瑾聽到他走得越來越近，然後
——盜夢室的門忽然燒起來。「呀！
你是來尋找你的夢的。你現在便永
遠不能離開這兒了！哈哈！」他怒
吼著，走向美瑾。

Megan heard him coming nearer and
nearer and then - the door of the Dream
Room burst into flames.
"So, you came looking for your dream.
Now you will never leave here. Ha Ha!"
he howled as he ran towards Megan.

「繩索，往上去！」美瑾指揮說，它 將美瑾舉
到窗台上。她迅速地撒出一些星塵，並大聲
叫道：「我許願希望有一條小徑帶我回家。」
她跳到小徑上，跑呀，跑⋯⋯

"Up rope!" Megan commanded and it
lifted her onto the windowsill. She quickly
threw some stardust and shouted,
"I wish for a path to take me home."
She jumped onto the path and ran and
ran...

…但是盜夢者總是在後面不遠處。

…but the Dreamstealer was never far behind.

當星塵在風中飄動時，美瑾說：「我許願希望盜夢者被鎖起來，
直至他答應永遠不再偷夢。」

With the stardust drifting in the wind, Megan said, "I wish the
Dreamstealer is locked away until he promises never
to steal dreams again."

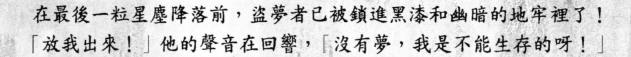

在最後一粒星塵降落前，盜夢者已被鎖進黑漆和幽暗的地牢裡了！
「放我出來！」他的聲音在回響，「沒有夢，我是不能生存的呀！」

And before the last of the stardust had fallen,
the Dreamstealer was locked in a dark and gloomy dungeon!
"Let me out!" his voice echoed.
"I cannot live without dreams!"

「但你偷了我們的夢啊！」美瑾哭叫著跑往她的家。

"But YOU stole OUR dreams!" Megan cried as she ran towards home.

阿班娜正在等候著她。「你有沒有將你的夢取回？」
她問道。
「有，我還把很多其他的夢放走啊！但是，
阿班娜，盜夢者會怎樣？」美瑾問道，「他
好像很悲哀似的，你要幫他，讓他能擁
有自己的夢，那麼他便不用偷別人的
夢了。」
「那麼便要看他是否真正後悔了，
我或者會幫他的。」阿班娜說。

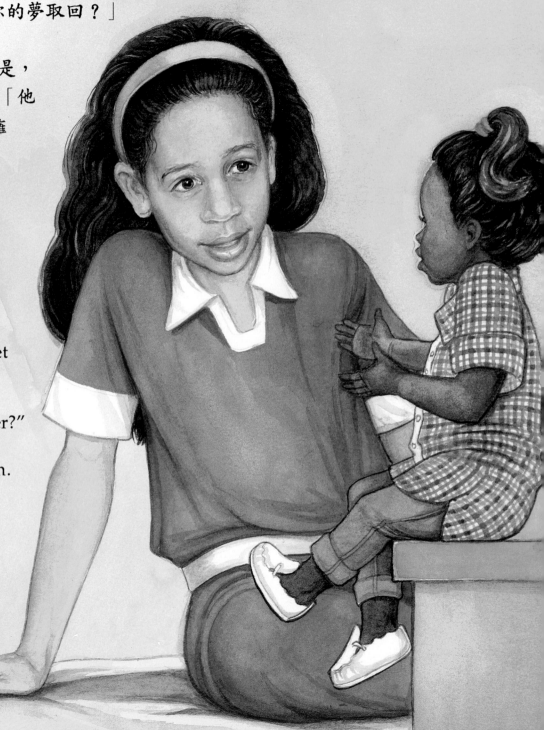

Abena was waiting for her. "Did you get
your dream back?" she asked.
"Yes and I set many others free as well!
But Abena, what about the Dreamstealer?"
Megan asked. "He looked so sad, you
have to help him to have his own dream.
Then he won't need to steal other
people's dreams."
"Well, if he's sorry for true,
I *might* help him," said Abena.

就在那時，美瑾的媽媽走進睡房。「你似乎好多了，」她說著，給美瑾一個緊緊的擁抱。
「造了個甜蜜的夢嗎？」
美瑾望一下阿班娜，只是微笑。

Just then, Megan's Mum came into the bedroom.
"You look much better," she said,
giving Megan a tight hug.
"Sweet dreams?"
Megan glanced at Abena
and just smiled.

To Jonathan, James and Sinead - E.L.
For Sarah and Eva, Robyn and Eliza - M.R.

Litho originations by Reprospeed Ltd, London
Printed in Hong Kong by South China Printing Co. (1988) Ltd.

Mantra Publishing Ltd
5 Alexandra Grove
London N12 8NU
Great Britain
Tel: 0181 445 5123

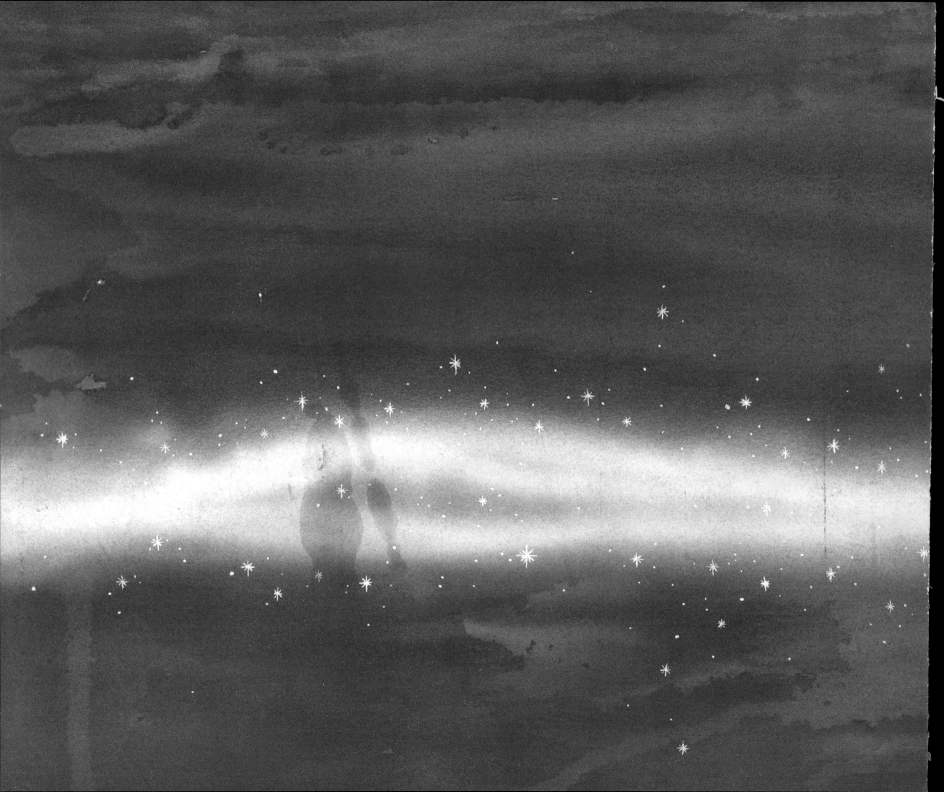